FRANKIE AND THE WORLD CUP CARNIVAL

BY FRANK LAMPARD

RANKIE AND THE WORLD CUP CARNIVAL

FRANK LAMPARD

SCHOLASTIC INC.

All rights reserved. Published by Scholastic Inc., 557 Broadway, New York, New York 10012, *Publishers since 1920*. SCHOLASTIC and associated logos are trademarks and/or registered trademarks of Scholastic Inc. Published by arrangement with Little, Brown Books for Young Readers.

The publisher does not have any control over and does not assume any responsibility for author or third-party websites or their content.

This book is a work of fiction. Names, characters, places, and incidents are either the product of the author's imagination or are used fictitiously, and any resemblance to actual persons, living or dead, business establishments, events, or locales is entirely coincidental.

ISBN 978-1-338-08910-3

10 9 8 7 6 5 4 3 2   16 17 18 19 20

Printed in the U.S.A.   40
First printing 2016

To my mom, Pat, who encouraged me to do my homework in between kicking a ball all around the house, and is still with me every step of the way.

Welcome to a fantastic
fantasy league—the greatest
soccer competition ever held
in this world or any other!

You'll need four on a team,
so choose carefully. This is a lot
more serious than a game in the
park. You'll never know who your
next opponents will be, or
where you'll face them.

So lace up your cleats, players,
and good luck! The whistle's
about to blow!

The Ref

PART ONE

CHAPTER 1

"Move over!" said Louise as she
came into the living room, carrying
a bowl of chips. Frankie shifted
along the couch, pressing right up
against Charlie.

"I can't go any farther," grumbled
Charlie, pointing with his goalie
gloves to Max, Frankie's pet dog.

He was curled up at the end of the sofa, asleep. "I thought dogs slept in baskets, anyway."

Max opened one eye and growled softly.

"Not *that* dog," said Frankie, laughing. "He just wants to watch the game with the rest of us."

"He's asleep!" said Charlie.

It was halftime in the World Cup Semifinal, and England was one-all with Argentina. At stake was a place in the Final against Brazil, where the tournament was taking place. Frankie had to pinch himself—no one had thought England would get this far. Especially not his dad. He'd booked a table at a fancy restaurant for himself and Frankie's mom on the night of the semifinal. He'd never thought he might actually miss an England game!

Which meant there was more room on the sofa for Frankie and his friends.

Charlie was trying to get a chip from the bowl, but he was struggling to pick one up.

"Why not take your gloves off?" said Frankie, knowing what the answer would be.

"No can do," said Charlie. "A goalkeeper's always got to be ready."

Frankie and Louise shared a

smile. Sometimes Charlie took things too far.

The TV was showing a replay of the other semifinal between Brazil and Germany. The game had been won when Ricardo, the nineteen-year-old Brazilian striker, had scored an incredible overhead kick in the last minute of the game. The fans were already calling it a "Ricardo." The TV showed the kick from several angles, normal speed and in slow motion. Frankie could only shake his head in amazement. The commentator was talking about how Ricardo had grown up very poor, living in a single room with his four sisters.

"I wish I could score a goal like that," said Frankie.

"I bet you could," said Louise.

Frankie shrugged. It was all very well scoring a great goal, but to do it in a game as important as a semifinal was another thing entirely.

"Imagine the pressure he was under!" said Charlie.

Frankie heard footsteps pounding down the stairs and his brother, Kevin, burst into the room wearing a new Brazil jersey. The only downside to his parents being out was that Kevin had to stay in to babysit.

"What's the score, babies?" he said.

He shoved Max onto the floor, then flopped on the sofa. Louise's bowl of chips spilled all over Charlie. Max grabbed a few from the carpet, then scampered back to his basket.

"It's one–all," said Frankie, trying not to get irritated. *Kevin's not much of a fan if he hasn't even watched the first half,* he thought.

Kevin snatched the remaining chips from Louise's lap and stuffed a handful into his mouth. "I bet England loses," he said. "They always lose."

Louise glared at him. "Come on, Frankie," she said. "Let's go kick the ball around out in the yard. There's still five minutes until the second half starts."

Charlie followed Louise through the French doors and into the yard, but first Frankie went to the back of the kitchen. In the cabinet under the sink were two balls. One was a few weeks old, and the other was a battered peeling wreck that barely bounced. Only a few people knew its secret. He grinned to himself, recalling all of the adventures they'd had, thanks to his magic soccer ball. Well, tonight he didn't want an adventure—he just wanted a quick game with his friends, then to get back for the second half. He took the good ball and closed the cabinet door.

It was a warm evening with clear blue skies. The neighborhood was quiet, with everyone indoors watching the game. Frankie bounced the ball a couple of times on his foot, then kicked it to Louise. She controlled it under her foot.

"Why not try that kick, Frankie?" she said. "I'll kick it up for you."

Frankie smiled. "Okay. You ready, Charlie?"

His friend had taken up position by the fence. The gap between two fence-posts was the goal they normally used.

"Always ready," said Charlie, spreading his gloves.

Louise chipped the ball into the air, and Frankie watched it sail toward him over his shoulder. At the last moment, he flicked his body backward.

"Loser!" shouted a voice.

Frankie's foot skimmed the ball and he landed in a heap on his back.

"Are you all right, Frankie?" asked Louise, rushing over.

Frankie rubbed his back, sitting up gingerly. His brother, Kevin, was at the back door, doubled over, laughing.

"He distracted me," said Frankie.

Kevin straightened up. "Always making excuses," he said. He disappeared for a moment, then returned carrying the magic ball. "Hey, you might have more luck with this one instead."

"Just be careful with it," said Frankie. He wished his brother had never found out about the ball's secret, but it was too late now.

"Why?" said Kevin, dribbling the ball into the garden. "Scared?"

"Of course not," said Frankie.

"Hey, freckle-face," shouted Kevin. "Save this."

He blasted the ball at Charlie, who caught the ball easily.

"Great save, Charlie," said Louise.

Kevin blushed. "Let me go again. I was just practicing with that one."

Frankie ran and retrieved the magic ball from beside the fence. He held it close to his chest. "That's enough," he said. "We shouldn't mess around with the ball. You know what it can do."

Kevin's shoulders sagged. "All right," he said. "You win."

He lunged forward suddenly and knocked the ball from Frankie's hands, then turned and kicked it hard. The fence shook as the ball bounced off of it.

"Why not play with the other ball?" said Charlie.

"I prefer this one," said Kevin. He swung his foot again.

Frankie couldn't do anything as the ball flew through the French doors and into the den.

CRASH!

CHAPTER 2

Kevin's face went white as he looked into the house.

Frankie glanced at his friends, hardly daring to go in and see what was broken.

A second later, Max trotted to the doorstep, his tail between his legs.

Frankie approached the French

doors slowly, and saw the TV lying on its side in the living room, with glass scattered across the carpet. He couldn't see the ball anywhere.

"Oh no!" said Louise.

"Nice one," said Charlie.

"It . . . it wasn't my fault," said Kevin.

Frankie felt dread building in the bottom of his stomach. His parents would be fuming. They were always telling him not to play soccer indoors.

"We'd better clean up the mess," he said quietly.

There were no more comments from Kevin as they swept up the

glass and set the TV upright again. Frankie couldn't help glancing at the clock on the wall. Two hours until his parents got back. More importantly, it was one minute until the second half began and now they had no TV to watch it on.

"We can go to my house if you want," said Charlie. "My mom will be watching her dancing show, but we have a spare TV in the garage."

"Thanks," said Louise.

"What about me?" asked Kevin.

Charlie looked long and hard at Frankie's brother, and Frankie expected him to say "no."

21

"All right," said Charlie. "Just promise not to break anything."

As Frankie was locking the back door, he couldn't help glancing at the TV. Perhaps he should call his mom now, just to let her know. He went to the phone hanging on the wall and dialed her number.

She picked up on the third ring. "What's wrong?" she said straight away. "Did Max swallow another golf ball?"

"No, Mom," said Frankie. "Max is fine."

In fact, Max was sniffing around the bottom of the TV, whining oddly.

"So what's the matter?" said his mom. "We've only just had our appetizers."

"There's been a little . . ." Frankie paused. Was it his imagination, or were there lights sparkling around the TV? ". . . accident," he finished.

Max was backing away.

"Accident?" said his mother, her voice shrill. "Is someone hurt? Where's Kevin?"

A picture was swimming in and out of focus on the remains of the cracked screen.

Frankie moved closer with the phone still clutched to his ear.

"Frankie?" said his mother. "Are you still there?"

More sparks, like tiny stars, were hovering in front of the TV. It wasn't an electrical surge. Frankie knew that much.

"It's Frankie," his mother was saying to his dad. "I don't know . . . an accident, he said . . ."

A face appeared on the screen— one that Frankie would have recognized anywhere.

"Ricardo!" he gasped.

"Pardon, but what is 'Ricardo'?" said his mother.

"Nothing, Mom," said Frankie. "Got to go."

He hung up the phone and approached the TV slowly. The Brazilian superstar was peering out. "Hello?" he said.

Is he talking to me? Frankie wondered.

By now, Charlie, Louise, and Kevin had come back into the room. "What's going on?" asked Louise. She did a double take at the TV. "Oh, it's working again."

"Is anyone there?" said Ricardo.

"We're here," said Frankie.

"This isn't possible," said Kevin. "The TV is *not* talking to us."

"*I'm* talking to you," said Ricardo. He held up the magic ball.

"I assume this belongs to one of you?"

"It's mine," said Frankie, holding up his hand.

Ricardo nodded, and pointed right at Frankie's face. "Right, do you have a team?"

Frankie looked at his friends. "Yes, but . . ."

"Come on, then," said the Brazilian. "I need your help."

"Come on where?" said Charlie.

"There isn't time to explain," said Ricardo. "The World Cup is at stake."

The hairs on Frankie's arms stood up. "How do we get to you?"

Ricardo shrugged. "How should I know? It's *your* ball!"

Max began rooting around on the sofa, getting his nose down the side of the cushion.

"Now isn't the time to be hunting for chips," said Charlie.

But when Max withdrew his nose, he was clutching the remote control.

It was sparkling, too. Frankie took it from him, and pointed it at the TV. "Here goes nothing," he said, and pressed the "On" button.

A sudden wind whipped through the room, tugging at his clothes. He heard a shriek and turned to see Louise with her hair lashing her face. Chips blew up around them, and Max's paws scrabbled on the carpet. Frankie realized he was being pulled toward the TV, and grabbed the edge of the sofa.

Kevin struggled across the floor, leaning into the wind. Charlie had latched his gloves around the doorframe.

With a bark, Max was lifted from the carpet and flew into the TV, vanishing in a silver flash.

Next Kevin shot past, arms flailing. He barreled into Louise and they both tumbled through the TV and disappeared. Only Frankie and Charlie remained.

"Don't fight it!" said Frankie, over the roaring rush of the gale. "Let go after three! One . . . two . . ."

Charlie hurtled past with a wail.

"Three!" Frankie said to himself. He let go of the couch and let the hurricane take him.

CHAPTER 3

The world went dark for a few seconds, then Frankie realized he could hear distant chanting. He could smell sweat and grass and leather.

He opened his eyes and found himself in a changing room, with shirts hanging on hooks, and other jerseys scattered on benches. His friends were all around him, their faces puzzled. Max gave himself a shake.

"Nice of you to join me," said a voice.

They all spun around and saw Ricardo standing behind them wearing a tracksuit and holding the magic soccer ball. Frankie couldn't believe he was there in the flesh.

"Hi," was all he managed to say.

Ricardo looked Frankie up and down, then glanced at the others. "You look very young to have the ball," he said.

"I won it at a fair," said Frankie, feeling a bit stupid.

"We've won every game we've played so far," said Louise, lifting her chin proudly.

"Best goalkeeping record in the fantasy league," added Charlie.

Max wagged his tail. "Toughest defense on four legs, too," he barked.

Frankie grinned—it was nice to have a *talking* dog again.

Kevin, for once, didn't say anything at all. He hadn't been a part of their team until today.

"Well, this challenge will be a lot tougher than anything you've faced before," said the Brazilian.

Frankie stepped forward. "We're ready. You said the World Cup was in trouble?"

Ricardo sagged onto a bench, placing the ball beside him. He nodded gravely. "Three items have been stolen," he said. "Without them, the Final will not happen."

"What are they?" asked Charlie.

Ricardo counted them off on his fingers. "The head referee's whistle, the ball that will kick off the Final, and, last of all, the trophy itself."

"Can't you call the police?" asked Kevin.

The Brazilian laughed emptily. "The police can't help with this," he said. "A magical problem requires a magical solution."

"So can't they just find another ball and another whistle?" said Kevin.

Ricardo shook his head. "You don't understand. These objects aren't just *things*. They have magical properties. The ball gives the players skills, the whistle ensures fair play, and the trophy—that's the most important of the three—is the spirit of soccer itself, the object which drives teams to win."

Kevin scoffed. "I don't believe it," he said.

Frankie glared at his brother, but Ricardo simply walked to the door. "Follow me, and I'll show you," he said.

As soon as he opened the door, Frankie heard the noise of the roaring crowd. "We're in a stadium, aren't we?"

Ricardo led them down a tunnel, and the noise grew louder. At the end, he pointed. "Not just any stadium."

Frankie rocked back on his heels as he saw the white shirts of the players on the field and the huge stands on all sides. "It's England and Argentina," he said. "We're in Brazil!"

The others huddled around him as they watched the second half of the game. The score was still one-all. But something was wrong. One player missed the ball completely and slid over. Another tripped over his own feet.

"The changes are happening already," said Ricardo. "They are losing their skills, you see?"

Two Argentine players jumped

for the same ball and banged heads. They lay on the ground, groaning. Then an England defender slid in for a tackle—on the referee! The crowd started to boo and hiss.

"Okay, even I believe you," said Kevin. "What can we do?"

As Ricardo took them back to the tunnel, Frankie felt despair growing in the pit of his stomach. *Four years of waiting for the World Cup are going to end in catastrophe unless I can do something about it.*

But this sounded far tougher than the other challenges they'd faced.

Back in the dressing room,

Ricardo pulled out a bag from beneath a bench, and opened it carefully. Inside were a pair of gold cleats. Frankie recognized them at once as Ricardo's. "These will take you where you need to go," he said. He handed them to Frankie.

Frankie turned the cleats over in his hands. "But they won't fit."

"Try them on," said the Brazilian with a faint smile.

Frankie pulled on the cleats, which were at least five sizes too big. "Told you," he said, as he laced them up.

"You'd better take this, too," said Ricardo, throwing the ball to Frankie.

As soon as he caught it, he felt the cleats tighten on his feet. They shrank in front of his eyes until they fit perfectly.

"Wow!" said Frankie.

"Hang on," said Charlie. "Why don't you recover the missing items?"

The Brazilian checked his watch. "Because," he said, "I'm due at a press conference in five minutes, then I have to see the trainer. I can't just vanish into thin air. The magic ball brought you guys here for a reason. It's up to you now."

Frankie's feet began to tingle. "Something's happening!" he said.

Ricardo took a step back. "Good luck, team," he said, and waved.

"Wait!" said Louise. "You never told us *who* stole the items."

Before Ricardo could answer, the dressing room vanished.

CHAPTER 4

Frankie found himself surrounded by looming trees. A canopy of branches above them blocked out most of the sun, but it was so hot that sweat prickled over his skin. Vines hung from the trees, wrapping themselves around the trunks. All around were colorful plants and huge ferns.

"This can't be right," he said. "Why are we in the jungle?"

"Maybe the cleats are broken," said Charlie, batting away a fly with his glove.

"It's the rain forest," said Louise. "The Amazon River flows through Brazil, remember?"

"Great!" said Kevin. "How are we supposed to get home?"

Max's ears pricked up. "Did you hear that?"

Louise shook her head. "Hear what?"

Frankie hadn't heard anything, either.

"That!" said Max. "I can't help it if dogs have more sensitive hearing than humans."

Then Frankie heard something, too. A distant, shrill sound. "A whistle!" he said.

"It's weird, aren't jungles supposed to be noisy?" said Charlie. "Where are all the animals?"

He was right. The rain forest was silent. The only sound Frankie

45

could hear was their own feet in the undergrowth.

And the whistle.

"It's coming from over there," he said to the others, pointing between the trees.

Max went first, nose to the ground. They climbed over the huge gnarled roots of the trees. The whistle grew louder. Frankie looked around. He couldn't help feeling that they were being watched. The forest was so dark he could only see a few feet ahead of him. Was that a shadow passing between the trees? He strained his eyes, but couldn't make anything out.

Eventually they reached a small clearing. The few branches overhead were loaded with green and orange mangoes. They were halfway across the clearing when Max stopped dead.

"What is it?" said Frankie.

A low growl sounded from the trees. "Uh-oh," said Charlie.

A set of yellow eyes peered from the gloom. Then another. "Double uh-oh," said Louise.

Pairs of eyes appeared all around them, then one by one, six or seven big black cats prowled into the clearing. Jaguars. Their teeth were as long as Frankie's fingers.

Charlie picked up a stick from the ground.

"Ooh, now I'm scared," said one of the jaguars, chuckling.

Frankie stood in front of his friends. "We don't mean you any harm," he said. "We're just here to find a whistle."

"Is that right?" said the jaguar. "Well, we have orders to eat anyone who's trying to find the whistle."

"You and your big mouth," muttered Kevin, shrinking even farther back.

Max puffed out his chest and stood as tall as he could—which was about up to Frankie's knees. "Orders from whom?"

"Never you mind," said the jaguar. "Any last requests?"

Frankie threw the ball up and kicked it as high as he could into the sky. It smacked into one of the branches, and hundreds of mangoes fell to the ground.

Thump! Thump–thump–thump!

The jaguars dodged this way and that as the fruits rained down.

"Run!" said Frankie.

They sprinted away from the big cats, plunging back into the forest. Frankie didn't even bother to look back—he knew the mango downpour wouldn't keep their enemies busy for long.

At last, panting for breath, they stopped behind a huge trunk.

"I think we lost them," said Louise. "Quick thinking, Captain!"

"But I also lost my magic ball," said Frankie.

"No, you didn't," said Charlie. He held up the ball in his gloves. "I caught it!"

Kevin emerged from the undergrowth last. He had mango stains down his shirt. "This will never come out!" he said.

"Better than being lunch, though," said a voice above them.

They all looked up to see a monkey sitting on a branch. "Hi," said Frankie.

"You should hide," he said, nervously. "Before Ali sees you."

The whistle blew again, and the monkey jumped to another branch. "Gotta go."

"Hey, wait!" said Frankie. But the hairy creature was gone.

More confused than ever, Frankie and his friends walked along the riverbank in the same direction as the monkey. *Who's Ali?* Frankie wondered. *Is he the one who stole the objects?*

Soon they came to a place where

the trees met the river, and one of the strangest sights Frankie had ever seen. Several alligators were lounging in the shallows, and beside each one sat a monkey holding a huge fern branch and using it as a fan. Parrots were waiting nearby and whenever a crocodile opened its mouth, one would peck at its dirty teeth. Some of the crocodiles were on their backs, while monkeys itched their bellies with sticks.

"I haven't seen a lot of wildlife shows," said Max, "but this doesn't look normal."

The alligators stirred together,

shifting their bulky bodies to make a channel between them. Frankie saw why—a huge alligator was heading toward them, gliding on the water. Weirdly, it wasn't using its tail to swim—it was being dragged by two snakes, their heads just above the water.

"That's seriously lazy," muttered Charlie.

Frankie felt a jolt of surprise as he saw that the massive alligator was wearing a cord over its ridged snout. "The whistle!" he whispered to his friends, pointing.

"How can we get it?" asked Charlie.

"Are those gloves bite-proof?" asked Kevin.

"Very funny," said Charlie.

"Maybe we can just reason with it," said Louise.

A low chuckle made them all spin around. The jaguars were back, covered in sticky pulp and looking unhappy. "Yes, you try reasoning with Ali," said the leader of the cats. "Now, move it!"

Frankie and his friends let the jaguars escort them to the shoreline of the river. The alligators turned one by one and watched them with cold stares. The one with the whistle was enjoying a back rub from two monkeys. *He must be Ali,* Frankie thought. *It's like he's got the whole jungle doing what he wants.*

"We found these intruders," said the jaguar. "They're looking for the whistle."

Ali bared his teeth in what might have been a smile. "Is that right?" he said.

"It was stolen," said Frankie, aware of all the teeth close by. "We've come to get it back."

"Well, in that case, I should just give it to you," said Ali.

"Really?" said Kevin.

"Er . . . not quite," said the alligator. "There's one condition—

you have to pass a test. A soccer
trial, to be precise."

"Do crocodiles play soccer?"
asked Max.

"Oh, how many times!" said Ali. "I
AM NOT A CROCODILE. Of course
crocodiles don't play soccer!"

"Sorry," said Max. "It's just you
look like a croco . . ."

Ali snapped his jaws. "So will you
accept the challenge?"

"Yes," said Frankie, without
hesitation.

Kevin grabbed his arm. "Wait!"
he whispered. "Don't you think you
should find out what the challenge
is first?"

"We don't have a choice," said Frankie. "You saw the England game. Someone could get injured if we don't get the whistle back and restore fair play."

"Right," said Ali. "Your job is simple. One of your teammates has to kick the ball across the river— from one bank to the other."

Frankie's heart sank as he gazed across the huge river.

"It's too far," said Charlie. "It's impossible."

"Not my problem," said the alligator. He was definitely smiling now. It was a very toothy grin.

CHAPTER 5

Frankie looked at his friends. *What have I agreed to?* he thought. *Charlie's right—the river is too wide. Even the England goalkeeper couldn't boot it that far!*

"You can have three tries," said Ali, "since I'm feeling generous."

"Let me try," said Kevin, grabbing

the ball from Charlie. "I've got the hardest kick."

He placed the ball on the ground, took a few steps back, then blasted it high. Frankie watched the ball sail across the water, then the wind caught it and it plopped into the river about halfway across.

"Rats," muttered Kevin.

"Not a good start," said Ali. He blew the whistle and one of the monkeys jumped into the water, swam to the ball, and brought it back.

More alligators had gathered in the water to watch, just their heads and backs breaking the surface. Frankie began to worry what would happen if they failed. The alligators looked hungry.

Louise stepped up next. She kicked the ball low, so the wind couldn't catch it. It skimmed across the surface a couple of times, but still fell short by about twenty feet. Charlie patted her on the back. "Good try," he said.

"Anyone hungry?" said Ali. "That little dog will do as an appetizer."

Max backed away. "Don't count your canines," he said. "We have one more try."

When the soaked monkey brought the ball back again, he

looked at Frankie sadly. "Good luck," he said. "We're all rooting for you."

"Yeah," squawked a parrot. "Since he got that whistle, he's been a terror. He's even got the sloths running around for him, and the sloths hate running *anywhere*."

Frankie narrowed his eyes. Seeing Louise's shot had given him an idea. "Hey, Ali," he said. "Maybe you should send all the other alligators away so they don't see you lose your bet."

The alligator rolled his eyes. "Really?" He chuckled. "Maybe I should call more, so they all see *you* lose."

Frankie shrugged and tried not to smile. "Go on, then."

Ali blew his whistle and the water swarmed with more alligators, snapping and thrashing. Soon the river was almost blocked with their bodies.

Frankie dropped the ball on the riverbank. He knew he'd only get one chance—this kick needed to be accurate.

"Let's get this over with," said Ali.

Frankie kicked the ball. It shot low over the water, then bounced on an alligator's head. Then it bounced again, and again, and again, ricocheting off the bridge

of reptiles. It skidded onto the far bank and Frankie's friends cheered. A few monkeys joined in, too, but they stopped when Ali blew his whistle.

"So can we have the whistle now?" said Frankie.

Ali narrowed his eyes. "No. You cheated."

He sank beneath the water,
and Frankie saw the shape of his
body swim off toward an island
in the middle of the river. The
other alligators vanished, leaving
Frankie and his companions on
the bank with the monkeys, the
jaguars, the parrots, and the
snakes.

"What now?" said Max.

Frankie clenched his fists. He
hadn't cheated. He'd used his brain.
Well, if the alligator won't give me
what he promised, I'll have to take it
for myself.

He glanced at the animals. "Do
you want your lives back?" he said.

"Yes!" chorused the animals.

"Then we need your help," said Frankie.

"Anything," said a monkey.

Frankie grinned. "Time to put Plan B into action!"

The jaguars had dragged the fallen branches over in their jaws, and the monkeys had found the vines to tie them together. It hadn't taken the friends long to make a raft. Now, Frankie and his friends used their hands to paddle toward Alligator Island. It was hard to fight against the current, and they were all breathing hard.

"I hope you know what you're doing," said Kevin.

So do I, thought Frankie. *If the snakes don't do their part, we'll be dinner.*

Ali and his friends saw them approaching, and waddled to where their island sloped into the water. "I told you," he said. "You're not getting the whistle. Now go away."

Frankie stepped off his raft into the shallows, as close as he dared. "You owe me," he said.

Ali shook his head. "Last warning," he said. "My stomach's rumbling and that means you've got about ten seconds."

The other alligators all dragged their bodies to the water's edge, licking their lips.

"I'm not scared of you," said Frankie, although, beneath the water, his knees were trembling.

"You should be," said Ali. With a flick of his tail, he surged into the water with his teeth bared. The others followed. Frankie scrambled back toward the raft, and Louise and Charlie grabbed his arms and pulled him onboard.

The next moment, the alligators all came to the surface. But they weren't snapping their jaws anymore. Each one had a snake coiled around their snouts, clamping their mouths closed.

The snakes had done it! Frankie's plan was working! Ali thrashed and made a lot of "Mmmm!" sounds, but a large snake gripped him tightly. A parrot swooped down from above, gripped the whistle's cord, and tugged it off. The bird flew straight up, then dropped it.

Straight toward the water.

"No!" yelled Frankie. It would sink without a trace.

Charlie's gloved hand reached from the side of the raft and snatched the whistle.

"Always ready!" said Louise.

But Charlie's lunge had rocked the raft away from the island, into the current. Suddenly they were spinning away into the fastest part of the river.

Frankie struggled to hold on as the spray splashed over the raft. Max lay on his belly. "I feel seasick!" he whined.

Everyone's faces were twisted in panic as the out-of-control raft surged down the river. Frankie tried to paddle, but he had no chance. They dipped and rose on the rapids, hanging on for dear life.

"What's that?" said Kevin, pointing downriver, drenched to the skin already.

Frankie followed his gaze and swallowed hard. Up ahead, the water seemed to vanish. This could mean only one thing.

"Paddle backward, all of you!" said Frankie. "It's a waterfall!"

They all leapt to the edges of the raft and began frantically cupping water, trying to slow themselves down. But it was hopeless. Slowly but surely, the current tugged them toward the drop.

They reached the edge, and as the makeshift boat began to dip, Frankie saw a drop of hundreds of feet below where the river plunged into a foaming cascade. His

stomach yo-yoed up to his throat
as gravity took hold.

Frankie closed his eyes and
clutched the whistle tightly. Was it
all over?

PART TWO

CHAPTER 6

"You guys look soaked!" said
Ricardo.

Frankie opened his eyes and
found himself and his friends in a
small room. The Brazilian was lying
on a table on his stomach, with one
leg of his tracksuit bottoms rolled
up. Frankie realized it was a training

room—he remembered that Ricardo had picked up a minor strain in his semifinal match.

Max shook himself vigorously, soaking the player.

"You'd be wet, too, if you'd almost drowned in the Amazon," he said.

The magic must have saved their skins, just in time.

"We rescued this," said Frankie. He opened his fist and held the whistle by its cord. Ricardo leapt off the bench.

"Good job!" he said. "I should never have doubted you!"

"Did you doubt us?" asked Charlie, frowning.

Ricardo smiled lopsidedly. "Only a little."

"Listen," said Louise. "What's really going on here? Who actually took these things?"

"There isn't much time, but I can tell you a little bit," said Ricardo. He clicked his fingers toward a TV on the wall and the screen blinked on. It showed a huge house on a hill, with sprawling lawns all around. There was an artificial field to one side, and a boy was doing tricks with a soccer ball, his feet a blur as he bounced it up and down, catching it behind his head and doing stepovers.

"Is that you?" asked Kevin. "I thought you grew up in the city?"

Ricardo shook his head. "That is Diego," he said. "He had a very different upbringing than me, as you can see. While I played barefoot, using sweatshirts for goalposts, he had everything he could ever wish for. His own field, the best equipment, even a coach.

His parents were very wealthy. Diego was always the best."

"I've never heard of him," said Frankie.

"That's because he stopped practicing," said Ricardo. "He used to call me names when I stayed later than everyone else to work on my technique. He knew there was something special about my soccer ball." He pointed to the magic ball in Louise's hands. "But by the time we tried out for the under–16 team, Diego had grown lazy. I was selected ahead of him."

"Wait—you had the magic soccer ball?" said Charlie.

The Brazilian nodded. "Diego was jealous and he stole the ball from me. He became lost in the magical soccer ball world for over two years, playing games through history and all over the world!"

"Until now," said Louise.

Ricardo nodded. "He must have found a way out, and he wants his revenge against the game."

"More importantly," said Kevin, "how is England doing?"

"Let's see, shall we?" said Ricardo. He clicked his fingers again and the TV switched channels to the England game. Frankie saw that there were only five minutes left and the score was still one—one. Not only that, but half the crowd seemed to have gone home. Two players were lying on the field injured, and, as they watched, an Argentine defender flattened the England striker right in front of the goal. The ref blew his whistle and pointed to the penalty spot.

"*Yes!*" said Frankie. "We have to win now."

The England striker picked himself up, and placed his ball on the spot.

Frankie sensed the whole room holding its breath with him as the striker jogged forward, swung his foot . . .

. . . and kicked the ball high over the goal.

Max groaned.

"England won't get to the Final playing like that," said Louise.

"Don't you see?" said Ricardo. "Fair play has been restored, but until you find the game ball, the players have no skills. And there won't *be* a Final, unless you can find the trophy."

Frankie's cleats began to tingle again. "Something's happening," he said.

He heard footsteps outside the

door. "Quick, my trainer's coming back!" said Ricardo.

As the door handle turned, the room vanished.

Frankie found himself surrounded by dancing people. Drums boomed and maracas clacked and horns blasted all around him. Max scampered between his ankles to avoid getting stepped on.

"We're at a carnival!" said Louise. "We must be in Rio de Janeiro!"

The river of people was slowly making its way down the street, and it was hard for Frankie to even stay close to his companions. They pushed their way toward the pavement. The road they were on led down to the beach and the sea, where lights sparkled on the water. People were wearing incredible costumes in every color under the sun. Huge floats rolled down the street as well, with more people dancing on top of them, or throwing sparkling confetti over the sides. Some had acrobats doing flips, or jumping up in the splits.

Normally, Frankie would have loved it, but today there was a more pressing matter.

How are we ever going to find the trophy or the ball here? There must be thousands of people!

Then he saw it. Coming toward them was a float shaped like a giant soccer ball. A juggler on stilts walked in front of it, tossing soccer balls into the air. As the float moved past, Frankie saw that a section of the huge orb was cut away, and sitting inside was a skinny young man in a pristine white tracksuit. He had slicked-back dark hair and he was sipping on a drink in a coconut shell. Gold rings covered his fingers. His face was set in a scowl.

Frankie peered closer. "That's Diego!" he said.

CHAPTER 7

"He looks like the only person not enjoying the carnival," said Louise.

"Makes sense," said Charlie.

"We need to get onboard."

They followed the float, which was moving at a slow walking pace, then clambered onto the back. Max was too small to climb up, so Frankie tossed him up to Charlie, and hopped onboard himself. No one seemed to notice them getting on—everyone was having too much fun. Frankie kept his eyes peeled for traps as he crept forward. *It can't be this easy . . .*

Diego had his back to them, but Frankie spotted a ball under his left foot. It was definitely a World Cup ball, with green, blue, and orange swirls. Perhaps the trophy was here, too, and they could get both things at the same time.

Frankie turned to his friends and put a finger to his lips. If they could stay quiet, he might be able to sneak up and . . .

"Did little Ricardihno send you?" said Diego, without turning around.

Frankie stopped. "Your game has gone on long enough," he said.

Diego pressed a button in the arm of his chair and it revolved to face Frankie. He tossed his drink aside, wiping a sleeve across his mouth. "This isn't a game," he sneered. "It's a war—a war against soccer!"

Frankie approached slowly, keeping his eye on the ball.

"I see my old friend has gotten

only the best to come after me," he said sarcastically. "A bunch of kids— pathetic!"

Frankie sensed his friends fanning out behind him. "Give us the ball," said Louise.

"Come and get it," said Diego.

Max darted out from behind Frankie's legs, and tried to clamp his teeth over the ball. Diego pressed a button on the arm of his throne, and a net shot up from the floor, closing over the dog. He rolled over several times, hopelessly tangled and barking madly. "Silly mutt!" said Diego. "Who's next?"

Louise ran at him, and Diego
pressed another button. Some sort
of liquid shot from the underside of
his seat, and Louise skidded. She
winced in pain and clutched her
ankle.

"Oil!" she said.

"I learned a few tricks, trapped in
that world for so long," said Diego.

Charlie, Frankie noticed, was sneaking up from the other side. Diego pressed another button and a blast of fire surged toward him. Charlie backed away, gloves in front of his face. The crowd around the float oohed and aahed. *They think it's all a show,* thought Frankie.

Charlie took off his gloves and stamped the fire out. His face was pale with anger. "I can't believe you made me take my gloves off!" he said. "I *never* take my gloves off."

"Maybe it's time you left me alone," said Diego. "Before someone gets hurt."

Frankie didn't dare take a step closer. Who knew what other tricks Diego had up his sleeve?

"Hey, look what I found!" called Kevin. Frankie turned and saw his brother poking his head through a hatch in the float.

"No! Get away from there!" shouted Diego.

"What is it?" called Frankie.

Suddenly the whole float rocked forward sharply, throwing Frankie off his feet. Diego tumbled from the chair, landing on his ball.

"The brake lever!" said Kevin.

The float began to rumble more quickly down the street. Kevin had let off all the brakes and now the float could travel fast—too fast. People screamed as they tried to scramble out of the way. The juggler fell from his stilts, landing on an awning above a store. His soccer balls bounced off down the street among the panicking carnival-goers. The float picked up even more speed, surging down toward the beach. Someone was going to get flattened.

"Stop it!" screamed Louise.

"Okay, okay!" said Kevin, ducking down again.

With a deafening screech, the float shuddered to a halt, sliding sideways. Frankie saw the ball roll free of Diego's grip and drop off the edge of the float into the seething crowd.

"Get the ball!" he shouted to his friends. He leapt off the float, landing in a crouch on the ground. He saw the ball bouncing back and forth between hundreds of pairs of feet. Louise climbed down after him, limping slightly and helped by Kevin. Charlie was untangling Max from the net.

"Sorry," said Kevin. "I thought if I caused a distraction . . ."

"You certainly did that!" said Louise.

Diego jumped over their heads and ran after the ball. Frankie was hot on his heels.

"You'll never beat me!" Diego shouted over his shoulder. He dropped into a slide, tripping several people as he reached the ball. "Ha!" he cried. He picked up the ball and ran off toward the beach.

Frankie sprinted in pursuit across the sand. Diego was quick at first, but soon he was panting. *Should've practiced more,* thought Frankie. Eventually, Diego stopped to face Frankie, glaring defiantly. "You'll never have the ball!" he said. He turned to the sea, and kicked the ball so far out into the water that Frankie couldn't even see it anymore.

Diego gave Frankie a cruel grin, but then his face fell. "What?" he said, looking left and right.

Frankie spun around and saw that his friends had arrived, and they all had a different ball at their feet. *Of course!* thought Frankie. *The juggler dropped them all!*

"So which one is the real one?" said Kevin. "They all look the same to me."

"This one!" said Ricardo. He strode down the beach, holding a ball. "I hope you don't mind. I

managed to slip away from my
hotel."

"You!" hissed Diego.

"Hello, old friend," said Ricardo.

Diego kicked the sand. "We're
not friends. You *stole* my place
on the team. You *left* me in that
fantasy world."

"You know that isn't true," said
Ricardo. He faced Frankie and his
friends. "Thank you. By the way—
England just won with an amazing
header in overtime. They're through
to the Final."

"Hurray!" said Louise. She threw
her arms around Charlie, who
blushed.

"You took *everything* from me," said Diego, "but you won't have . . . THIS!"

With a flash of light, the golden trophy appeared in his hand.

CHAPTER 8

Frankie stared. "Is that the real World Cup?"

"It's *my* real World Cup," said Diego.

"It's for real *winners*, not thieves," said Ricardo.

Diego's face darkened. "What have you ever won?" he said. "It's time to see who's really the best. I'll

give you the trophy if you and your team can beat me and mine. That sounds fair, right?"

Ricardo looked at Frankie and his friends, biting his lip. "I don't know . . ."

"We'll do it," said Frankie. "But where is *your* team?"

Diego grinned. "They're coming," he said. He held the World Cup over his head and gold rays of light shot from the top. As they hit the sand, shapes began to appear—the outlines of figures. Frankie looked around to see if anyone was watching, but the beach was deserted apart from them. As the golden light faded away, five players stood beside Diego.

"Meet my team," he said. He pointed first to a boy—"This is Tanaki." Next came a girl with long blonde hair. "And Hanna, from Germany." Then two stocky, identical dark-skinned boys stepped up, folding their arms. "Meet Xander and Benji," said Diego. Last of all was a girl at least six feet tall. "And my goalkeeper, from the USA, Mindy."

None of the opposing players said a word—and from the blank look in their eyes, Frankie guessed something weird was going on. It was like they were robots.

"Where did you find this team of yours?" asked Louise.

Diego shrugged. "These are all the previous owners of the magic soccer ball," he said. "The best of their generations. You want to earn the trophy, these are the players you have to beat."

"Now wait a minute, Diego . . . ," said Ricardo.

"The game will be sudden death," said Diego, as his players spread out behind him. Frankie realized it was six on a side, which suited him fine. *We have Ricardo, after all!* Goalposts had magically sprouted from the sand at opposite ends of the beach, and Mindy took her place between one set. Charlie ran to the other, kicking up sand as he went. Frankie realized he wasn't wearing his gloves.

Frankie pointed to both wings, and Louise and Max took up their positions. Kevin stood in front of Charlie's goal, ready to defend.

"Come on!" said Frankie to Ricardo. "We need you up front."

Ricardo shook his head. "I can't play."

"*What?*" said all of Frankie's team at the same time.

"I just . . . don't feel like it," said Ricardo. "Plus, what if I get injured?"

Frankie couldn't believe what he was hearing.

"You brought us here," said Kevin. "What's the matter with you? The World Cup is at stake!"

Diego chuckled. "Don't you get it?" he said. "His spirit has gone. He doesn't care anymore. Now, ready to start?"

"But we only have five players," said Louise.

"I know," said Diego, with a sly grin. "I'll let you kick off, since you have the ball."

Frankie looked down at his feet, where the magic soccer ball rested on the sand. He had one chance to save the World Cup.

And he wasn't going to blow it.

He passed the ball sideways to Louise, but it skidded, then died on the loose sand. Hanna pounced on it quickly, chipped the ball over Louise's tackle, then lofted the ball toward Tanaki. It was way too high for Max, and Tanaki met it with his head, leaping above Kevin, and powering a shot toward Charlie's goal. Frankie watched with his heart in his mouth as Charlie dived.

Slap!

He saved it with his palm. Charlie rubbed his hand. "Ouch!"

"Nice work!" Frankie shouted, as he rushed back to the goal, but he thought, *That was too close! We almost lost in the first few seconds.*

Louise came over to him and Max joined the huddle, too, while Kevin trudged over, looking glum. "We can't play along the ground like we do at home," she said. "We need to adapt."

"But how?" said Frankie. "We don't stand a chance."

Louise gripped his arm. "You can't

think like that, Frankie," she said.
"You can't lose your spirit, too."

"But they have one more player
than us," said Frankie. "And you
heard what Diego said. These guys
are the best."

"No," said Max, by his feet.
"Remember all the times we've
pulled through."

"That's right," said Charlie. "We
need you to be our captain and lead
from the front."

Frankie smiled at his friends.
"Okay," he said, feeling a flicker of
hope. "Let's try and keep the ball in
the air."

Charlie tossed it out, and Max

headed it to Louise. She let the ball bounce.

"To me, Louise," Frankie shouted.

She dinked the ball neatly over both of the twins, Xander and Benji. Frankie controlled it on his chest, then his knee. It was going perfectly. He saw Tanaki heading his way, and adjusted his body for the shot on goal.

Thump! Suddenly his feet were hit out from underneath him, and Frankie hit the sand hard, the wind knocked out of his lungs. He lay on his side, struggling to breathe, as Diego took the ball and darted upfield. He skipped

around first Louise, then Max, then Kevin, leaving them all trailing. He was one-on-one with Charlie. Charlie rushed out, spreading his arms, but Diego just rolled the ball between his legs. It slid into the open goal.

Diego slid onto the sand, his arms in the air. "I won! I won!" he cried.

"No, you didn't," said Hanna.

Frankie frowned as he picked himself up.

"Yes, I did," said Diego. "Look, the ball is in the goal."

"You fouled the opposition," said Tanaki.

Diego grabbed the ball. "I didn't summon you here for your opinions," he said.

Mindy stepped out of the goal. "Well, we're not cheats," she said. "It's a free kick to them."

Diego faced his team, and Frankie. "Fine," he said. "Let's play your way." He kicked the ball angrily back to Frankie, who set it down where the foul had happened.

"Let me take it," said Kevin.

"Frankie should take it," said Louise. "He's the captain."

Kevin stood over the ball. "Frankie's lost it," he said harshly.

"You heard him. He doesn't think we can win."

Diego walked over. "I don't care who takes it," he said. "Just get on with it."

Louise was muttering something to Kevin under her breath. To Frankie's surprise, she looked sideways at him and nodded. "You're right, Kev," she said. "You should take it."

Max lay on the sand, hiding his face in his paws. Charlie's shoulders sagged.

Frankie's heart sank like a stone.

Even Louise doesn't believe in me anymore. None of my team does.

CHAPTER 9

Frankie stepped away from the ball.
It was all up to his brother now.
The other team had formed a wall
in front of the goal and Mindy was
jumping up and down on the goal
line. There was no way Kevin could
score.

"Hey, Frankenstein," said Kevin.

"Remember in the garden, before the TV broke, when we were practicing and you missed the kick?"

Frankie nodded. *Of course I missed*, he thought sadly. *I should never even have tried.*

"I distracted you on purpose," said Kevin. "I . . . I knew you could do it, and I was just jealous. Because . . ." he took a deep breath. "Because you're better than me. You always have been."

Frankie could hardly believe what he was hearing. *Is my brother actually being nice to me?*

"Yeah," said Louise, with a wink.

"We *all* know you can do that kick, Frankie."

Max ran up to Frankie's leg. "Show 'em how it's done, boss," he whispered.

Frankie understood what he had to do. It was a risky plan, but it might be their only chance. He looked at Ricardo, who was standing at the water's edge. He'd put all his faith in Frankie's team. They couldn't let him down.

"Enough yapping!" said Diego.

Frankie began to walk back to his own goal, pretending to be defeated, but he watched out of the corner of his eye. As Kevin started his run-up, Frankie turned and ran at the goal. Instead of shooting, Kevin clipped the ball sideways.

"Huh?" said Diego.

Frankie watched the ball come over his shoulder, looping as if in slow motion. He flung himself into the air, jerking his hips up and bringing his leg around. He was upside down as his foot met the ball.

Whack!

As he landed in the sand, he squirmed around to see. Mindy was sprawled in front of her goal. Her wall of defenders was staring

backward. Frankie couldn't see the ball. Had he scored?

"SUPERGOOAAAAALLLL!" yelled Louise.

"You did it, bro!" said Kevin, leaping on top of him.

"Go, Frankie!" screamed Charlie, throwing himself onto the pile as well.

Through the gap in their limbs, Frankie saw Max spinning in happy circles on the sand.

As his friends rolled off of him, Frankie found himself staring at a pair of feet. Ricardo leaned down beside him and held out a hand. "I recognize that kick!" he said.

Frankie blushed. "It was a 'Ricardo,'" he said.

"It was better than mine," said the Brazilian. "Let's call it a 'Frankie' from now on."

Frankie took his hand and climbed to his feet. A flash of panic shot through his chest. "Where's Diego?" he said, staring down the deserted beach. "Where's his team?"

"I don't think he wanted to stick around," said Ricardo. "He always was a sore loser."

"But what about the World Cup trophy?" said Louise. "He ran off with it."

Frankie ran his hands through his hair. *After all that . . . we still haven't won the trophy . . .*

"No, he hasn't," said Charlie. "Look!"

A few feet away, Max was digging at the beach with his paws, kicking up sand. Frankie saw the glint of gold metal. "It's the trophy!" he said.

Max turned around. "You should be the first to hold it, Frankie," he said.

Frankie walked over slowly with his friends. The World Cup seemed to glow, even though it was half-covered in sand. Frankie crouched down and lifted the trophy, dusting it off. He had dreamed of holding it ever since he'd first played soccer as a little boy. *Can this really be happening?*

"Congratulations, Team Frankie," said Ricardo. "I couldn't have picked a more worthy side. Thanks to you, the World Cup is safe."

Frankie felt a strange shiver along his arm.

"To Team Frankie!" said Louise.

"To Team Frankie," cried his friends.

Silver lights cascaded around them like the stars were falling from the sky. Frankie hoisted the trophy into the air.

"To Team . . ."

"Frankie?" said his mother's voice. "We're home!"

Frankie was standing in his living room, with his friends at his side. His hand was empty. Any feeling of triumph sapped away. The TV was still propped up at an angle, the screen shattered. Kevin looked terrified. "Frankie?" called his mother again. "Kevin?"

Frankie ran to the door to intercept his parents, followed by the others.

In the hallway, his dad was taking off his coat. "What a bizarre game!" he said. "For a few minutes, it was like watching kids play!"

"Dad, there was an accident," Frankie began.

"Can't complain, I suppose," continued his father. "No one would have picked England for the Final, would they?"

Frankie's mother had frozen, staring into the lounge.

"I can explain," said Frankie.

His dad had seen the wrecked TV now, too. He turned to face Frankie. "Well, you'd better start right now," he said.

Frankie took a deep breath, and realized he couldn't think of a single thing to say.

Three days later, Frankie and Kevin were sitting in their bedroom,

feeling very sorry for themselves.
Frankie was fiddling with the dial
on his dad's old radio.

"I can't find it!" he said. "What's
the station?"

Max whined, not for the first
time that evening.

"This is *so* unfair," said Kevin. "I
can't believe we're not allowed to
watch the World Cup Final."

Frankie heard a crackle, then the
announcer's voice. *"And welcome
to Rio, for a night that hosts one of
the most eagerly anticipated games
for a generation. The Three Lions
take on the might of Brazil."*

The voice drifted into static again.

"I mean, you wait nearly fifty years for England to make the Final, and we're stuck up here without a TV to watch it on," grumbled Kevin.

Frankie could hardly blame his parents for grounding them. The TV was an expensive one, and now his dad had to go to his mother-in-law's to watch the game, and he didn't like that at all! Charlie had said he'd record the game anyway, so they could watch it another time. They had to be content with the radio.

"... *and there it is,*" said the announcer. "*The trophy both teams*

are playing for. The most famous
reward in the world of sports . . ."

Frankie smiled to himself,
imagining the World Cup being
shown on-screen. To think,
just three days ago he'd won it
himself!

"I doubt we'll ever get a chance
again," Kevin said. "Or if we do,
we'll be so ancient we can't play
anymore . . ."

"What are you guys doing in your
bedroom?" said the radio.

Max's ears pricked up and
Frankie bolted upright.

"Was that Ricardo's voice?" said
Frankie's brother.

"*It should be,*" said the Brazilian. "*Because it is me.*"

Frankie turned the radio volume up. "Hello?" he said. "Where are you?"

"*I'm in the tunnel,*" said Ricardo. "*About to go onto the field for the World Cup Final. I just remembered I forgot to give you something.*"

"What?" said Frankie, feeling foolish for talking to a radio.

"*Your VIP tickets,*" said the voice.

Frankie's bedroom vanished, and his stomach flipped as he found himself high in the packed stands overlooking a bright green field. The noise around him was deafening—thousands of fans chanting and singing and blowing horns. Kevin was sitting on one side, Louise and Charlie on the other. "We're really here, aren't we?" said Louise. "At the World Cup Final."

"Will someone lift me up so I can actually see?" said a voice.

Frankie looked down and saw a furry face peering out beneath his seat. He placed Max on his lap. "There you go, boy."

"Er . . . how did that happen?" asked Charlie. Frankie grinned to see he was wearing a new pair of gloves.

The teams were coming out onto the field, England in their red away uniforms, Brazil in yellow and blue. A player halfway along the Brazilian line turned to them and waved. It was their friend, Ricardo.

"We were sent a special invite," said Frankie, waving back. "One last bit of magic."

The best magic they'd seen so far!